GOOD MORNING, GRIZZLE GRUMP!

By Aaron Blecha

HARPER
An Imprint of HarperCollinsPublishers

Library of Congress Control Number: 2015958386

ISBN 978-0-06-229749-5

The artist used Prismacolor Col-Erase Carmine Red and Blue pencils on
Strathmore Bristol Vellum to create the illustrations for this book.
Typography by Rachel Zegar. Hand lettering by Aaron Blecha.

16 17 18 19 20 SCP 10 9 8 7 6 5 4 3 2 1

❖

First Edition

All the animals of the forest have awoken from their
winter slumber and are joyfully welcoming spring.
All the animals, except for one. . . .

Grizzle Grump is hungry. He stomps down the mountain in search of a springtime snack.

"AHA!

What's that delicious smell
coming from these brambly bushes?"

BERRIES!

Gooseberries!

Lingonberries!

Boysenberries!

All ready to EAT!

Now, where
did Squirrel go?

Huckleberries!

HEE
HEE
HEE

With a
gurgling!
And a
gargling!

Grizzle Grump and his empty tummy stomp off in search of another springtime snack.

FISH!

Slimy FISH!

Slippery FISH!

Fast FISH!

All ready to EAT!

Now, where
did Squirrel go?

Flippery FISH!

HEE HEE HEE

With a
grumbling!
And a
rumbling!

Grizzle Grump and his empty tummy stomp off in search of another springtime snack.

With a
bubbling!

And a
burbling!

Grizzle Grump and his empty tummy stomp off in search of another springtime snack.

RUMBLE RUMBLE RUMBLE GARGLE RUMBLE GRUMBLE
GRUMBLE GURGLE GURGLE
GRUMBLE GURGLE GARGLE
GURGLE RUMBLE GURGLE
GARGLE
GRUMBLE RUMBLE GARGLE

Grizzle Grump searches high
and low, near and far, until . . .

SNIFF SNIFF SNUFFLE

AHA!

What's that delicious smell
coming from over that hilly hump?"

"Whew! All that eating has made me sleepy! I need a nap!"